THROUGH YOUR EYES

THROUGH YOUR

EYES

A NOVELA SERIES

SHANE GRAHAM

Paperback ISBN: 979-8-234-09459-9

For all Veterans,
but especially for my father.
Vietnam left a lot of scars,
but through my eyes Pop,
you were a hero.

As the rain pours down on the car, he takes one last deep breath. With no umbrella to cover him, just a hood over his head, and some sort of cloth over his mouth, he steps out of the car and walks with intent toward the house, a bag held in one hand. He stands on the front porch, almost staring at the ground as if bowing his head in prayer, too distracted to knock. After a moment has passed the door is finally opened by a meager looking woman, Joanne Locke.

"Oh. Hello. You must be…uh…him? Won't you come in?"

The man enters the house and gazes around the room, as if looking for something. Despite her letting this hooded figure into her home she seems quite hesitant about interacting with him.

"Can I get you something to drink? Or take your coat?"

For the first time they make eye contact and something causes her to wince in fear. The man, on the other hand, is as if he is staring right through her.

"Oh that's right. You don't talk until after. I'm sorry; I've never done something like this before. But when Sue Boland, we played Bunko together, told me about you and what you do. I thought you could help me."

He just keeps the stare on her.

"Right. Everything you asked for is in the basement. Everything." She stresses the last.

The man in the hood nods in approval, extends his hand, and is handed a plain brown envelope. He opens it to see a nice wad of cash, and then puts it in his bag before heading for the basement. He enters the room and sees his task ahead of him: Robert Locke, Joanne's husband, tied to a chair.

"Who the hell are you?" Robert demands.

As if that is the signal, the man removes his hood. Robert Locke stares in disbelief and fear at the masked man in his basement. He reads every detail about his mask: it's almost metallic looking, like its armor, the simplicity of the colors black and white, but the eyes of the mask are so mysterious.

Upon further inspection, they look more like goggles. Nothing can penetrate them: not light, not judgement, perhaps not even the emotions of others.

"Look, don't bother answering. You don't matter." Never has Robert had to summon so much courage to speak. "What matters is who I am. I'm Robert Locke. Street boss for the Higgins clan."

As Robert continues to ramble on, the masked man begins to set up an I-pod dock that was in his bag.

"What's with the speaker?"

The masked man gives no response.

"What, did those goombah Berlusconis put you up to this? Those pasta suckers will get their guns when we get our money."

The masked man pulls a sheet off of a table to reveal the tools Joanne had set up for him: a hammer, a set of pliers, a lighter, a belt, and a phone book. Each item he gently touches, stares at each item giving them the attention each one deserves, almost as if he's caressing a lover.

"What are you doing?" demands Locke. "What is all that?"

The masked man slowly turns his head and returns the stare at Locke.

"Answer me God damn it."

"Please don't take the Lord's name in vain in my presence." The masked man finally responds

"What?" asks Locke, more confused than ever.

"I know not everyone's beliefs are mine, and freedom of speech. But, we all have those red button things that just automatically send us over the edge. And that's mine."

"What the hell is going on?"

"Street boss for an Irish mob is pretty impressive. Too bad you can't add loving husband or caring father to that title. But you still can. Tell me where your son is, then let him and Joanne disappear."

"Oh God, my wife put you up to this? Look I'll tell you like I told that bitch, Ethan is my son. She wants to leave? Fine. I can't wait to see how she makes it on her own. Probably on her back. But my son is living with me. End of discussion"

"I think Joanne is concerned that you want Ethan to follow in your footsteps, which wouldn't be so bad if what you did wasn't, shall we say, morally questionable, not to mention you have a temper, and like to use your belt as a means of discipline.

I think Joanne is afraid you might use it on Ethan when he gets a little older."

"How I keep my family in line is none of your business."

"So Joanne called me" he says while ignoring him. "My job is to get information. Somehow, some way. In this case, the information is the location of your son. So, what do you say? Save us both time and aggravation, and just tell me where Ethan is."

Robert spits on the masked man, which is not too disgusting since his face is covered, but the insult remains.

"Well, step one is over", he says with great restraint.

"Step one of what?" asks Robert.

"Of getting the information. Step one is talking. Just asking in the slim chance it is that easy to get the information. It didn't work, so I'm afraid it's all physical from here."

"You don't have the balls to-"

"-You know, I'm still fairly new at this. Which you might think is a good thing, but it's not.

Torture is a very precise exercise. If I punch you in the head too hard, you turn into a vegetable. I cut one inch too far to the right or left and you bleed to death. And that is what's happening here Locke. You're about to be tortured. Let that sink in."

Robert begins to laugh at the idea that the masked man would have the courage to torture him.

With that, the masked man pulls out a switch blade knife and adds it to his tools, and the laughter fades.

"Do you have any questions?" asks the masked man as he takes off his coat.

The masked man pushes the play button on his remote to begin the song 'Disturbia' by Rhianna, which causes Robert to laugh, more out of confusion than arrogance.

"What's the matter, no Whitney Houston?" Robert says through the laughter. But the laughter stops when the masked man back

hands Robert.

"Where are you hiding Ethan?" he asks Robert somewhat calmly.

"Do you know who I am?" Robert says with a scary tone.

The masked man slaps him again and has a vision of a young boy screaming, but shakes it off.

"We've already established that," the masked man yells. "Robert Locke, Street boss, blah blah blah. But what I want to know is where Ethan is."

"He's my son, he needs a father in his life," Robert is stopped by a punch to his face. "Ow. You touch me again, you're dead." Without missing a beat the masked man hits him in the head. "You never hit people in the head, I might forget things."

"You took that line from The Joker," the masked man says, unimpressed as he continues to hit him.

The blows come to a halt and the Masked Man appears to be soaking in the music as Rhianna sings the words 'bum-bum-bi-dum' before grabbing the belt.

"I heard that this is what you like to use on Joanne if she looked at another man, didn't have dinner ready on time, corrected you in front of your friends, or if you just felt like it. My dad used this on me once when I lied to him. Like this" the masked man wraps the belt around Robert's neck. "He said never be afraid to talk, because life will have many moments where you don't get to talk no matter how much you want to. So, I should talk when I get the chance. Joanne wants to give Ethan a normal life, and if you care about him, you will let her do that. I'm going to let you talk now, so I suggest you say what I want to hear."

He relinquishes the garrote's hold and watches Locke gasp for air.

"Whatever she's paying you, I'll double it", he says through the heavy breathing. "Just let me go."

The masked man drops the belt and grabs the pliers and goes right to pinching the space between his thumb and index finger. Robert screams in pain.

"You think I'm doing this for the money you arrogant son of a bitch? Feel that pain, Locke. It's nothing compared to the pain Joanne feels every night she spends away from her son. Where is Ethan?"

"Please let me go." Robert begs through unrepentant tears.

"Are you crying?" the masked man asks as he relinquishes the grip. "No. You don't get to cry. You either be a man and tell me to fuck off, or you be a better man and do the right thing. But stop crying."

Robert cannot seem to stop. He just continues to cry and sniffle.

"You know what? To hell with it. Wherever Ethan is, at least he'll be away from you." The masked man grabs the switch blade and puts it to Robert's neck.

"Ok. Ok. He's with my sister. She took him to New York City and they're staying at a Hilton. Please no more."

The song ends. Robert goes back to crying. What was only four minutes felt like an eternity for him. The masked man puts away the switch blade. He takes a minute and stares at Robert, and then proceeds to put his I-Pod and docking station in his bag, along with all the things Joanne gave him to torture with.

"Ok, it's almost over. Joanne will get Ethan and I'm sure by then one of your McFriends will come and get you. You did the right thing Robert."

He pats Robert on the shoulder and exits the basement, leaving him a wallowing mess tied to a chair.

He enters the family room to find Joanne sitting and waiting anxiously.

"Wow that was fast" says Joanne with much anticipation.

"Ethan is with Robert's sister in New York, at a Hilton Hotel."

"Ugh, she's a crack head on her best day. Well since I know now, I'll get him back and then get him away from this life."

"I'm glad for both of you. Can you handle the sister?"

"Yes. She'll just want a couple of bucks for her next fix. You can finish him off now."

"I'm sorry?"

"You can go kill him now."

"Um, I think you misunderstood what I do. I don't actually kill them; the threat of it is just a tactic I use. If that doesn't work, I will find another way to get the information out of them."

"You can't just let him walk around. What if he comes after us?"

"Well then you go kill him. A gun is like a computer mouse, just point and click. But I guarantee the mob will come after you if you kill one of their own. Right now he's just a guy that got beat up by some schmuck."

"What kind of a man are you?"

"What did you say?"

The masked man stares at her, and has a vision

of a woman crying. He exits the house with a slam of the door. Once again the rain is pouring down on the masked man, as he stares into his reflection in the car window. He looks up into the clouded sky and removes the mask and enjoys every drop that falls on his face.

"As I look up to the heavens, I open the windows to my soul and ask that you wash away my sins. Please forgive me for what I have done, and what I will do. May my life be an example of your justice. Amen."

Maintaining his weapons is his favorite thing to do while he waits for his son to come home. There is something about the sheer sound of sharpening his knife that distracts him from the absence of his son, as well as excites him. Just as the knife feels as sharp as before, his son pulls into the warehouse.

"How did it go?" he asks as his son steps out of the car.

"What do you think?" He tosses him the envelope filled with cash.

"Well done Michael."

"Thanks", he says through a sigh.

"What's wrong?"

"Nothing."

He knows when Michael is lying; after all he taught him everything he knows about reading people.

"He was a deadbeat Dad. Right?"

"Yeah."

"As I recall he abused his wife."

"That's right."

"So why do you look like someone just put down your dog?"

"I think he truly felt he was doing the right thing. That he was keeping his family in line."

"But he's not. What he's doing is not right. He's not being a good husband or father."

"Who are we to judge? We're just doing what we feel is right, but in the eyes of the law and society, we're the bad guys."

"Do not judge by appearances, but judge with right judgment. John 7:24. Do not forget my son; what we do is a service to others, but above all to God. We make sure justice is served."

"I know, Father."

"Then what's with you? I've never seen you like this after a job. You've never had a doubt."

"I just..." Michael stops himself, because, while he has a lot to say he doesn't want his Father to be disappointed. Like everyone else, there is that inner desire to please the ones who gave him life. "I just wish I was as sure as you. That I had the drive that you put into your work."

"No you don't, my son. Believe me, you don't want to see her face in every job you have. That's why I give my life to dispensing God's will."

Michael nods in agreement. He never thought of it like that. He just needs to remember that Father knows best.

"So" Father says to quickly change the mood. "What tactic did you use?"

"The 'I'm still new at this' followed by the giving up and just wanting to kill him."

"Aw, that was always one of my favorites. The look of fear in their eyes when they realize the man in front of them can't control his emotions and just might actually kill them" he says with a bit of a chuckle. "Of course I'm not too fond of your music selection. Give me classical music like Bach, Beethoven, and Wagner. True artists of sound."

"Hey, I've found that if the guys can't stand the music, it's just another form of irritation that will help us break them faster. It especially helps if they think they are big, tough, manly men."

"And was he one of those guys?"

"He thought I wouldn't have the balls to lay my hands on a street boss for the Irish mob" Michael says through laughter.

"Oh give me a break. See that's a problem with people today Michael. They rely too much on their titles, and not enough on their actions. That's what will always separate us from them."

"I get it. You're right."

"I'm always right," Father says with a hint of arrogance. "Oh, before I forget, we have an important meeting with a potential client tomorrow."

"Well, you always handle the clients. Just tell me who and what I have to get out of them-"

"-No this is different" he interrupts. "We would work for them full time."

"What?"

"They want to find someone to use in their digression."

"Hold on" Michael says with frustration. "You keep saying 'they'. Who are you talking about?"

"You'll find out at the meeting."

"Come on."

"I want you to keep an open mind. This can be huge for us. We don't have to worry about dry spells of business, clients coming to us, about getting caught."

Michael can't believe the words coming out of his Father's mouth.

"Since when is our job about the money"

"You know what I mean." Michael has to take a second to recover from this bomb his Father has dropped on him. "Michael," he continues "the harsh reality that men like us have to face is that we can't do this forever."

"I know that."

"Maybe. But in this line of work we have to live in the moment and I can't tell you how many guys decided to stay there. Who spent the whole time thinking about the guy they got the information from. Wondering if he was really a bad person, if they told the truth. Forgetting how important what they do is, but also forgetting about the future."

"So which are we?" Michael says with some smug.

"Neither. We are different. Because we remember that what we do is bigger than us, bigger than the moment."

Michael just stares at his Father. They both know that Michael is going to go along with this, but the question is whether or not he really has a choice.

"You promise that we'll still be doing God's justice?"

"Of course."

"And no innocents."

"Do you even have to ask."?

"I'm serious."

Michael grabs him with a little desperation.

"I promise."

Michael lets go and walks away. His Father keeps the stare at him, but then in one motion turns and throws the knife at the center of a hanging target.

"Why are you doing this?" she screams through the tears. "What kind of a man are you?"

And with that Michael wakes up in a cold sweat. Breathing hard, his heart beating so hard it feels like it is about to come out of his chest. Unfortunately this feeling is nothing new to him. Many times he has woken up from this flashback. Not a nightmare, but a flashback. A nightmare has potential to educate the person asleep from the events or symbols. From what Michael goes through, there is nothing to learn, only something to feel, guilt.

He lays his head on the pillow hoping to go back to sleep, but deep down he knows it is pointless with all the thoughts running through his head. His Father's news, on top of the events that transpired earlier, he knows he will just stare at the clock for the rest of the night. He figures he might as well make the most of his time by going out.

Walking along the shore always helps soothe Michael's soul. The clashing of the waves, smelling the salt in the air, and the moonlight shining down on the waves like it's right out of a Norman Rockwell painting. But this time it's his mind that's not at ease. So many questions about his work, his father, his means for getting justice. Too many questions to comprehend right now, at least on an empty stomach. A trip to the local cafe for a pastry and some coffee would hit the spot. It also doesn't hurt that there's a chance that she'll be there.

CHAPTER 4

They play the look away game every day at the coffee house: he stares at her but then looks away when she glances at him, and vice versa. She's playing hard to get. Hoping maybe he'll put a pause on the whole tall, dark, handsome and mysterious card, the mysterious part at least, and come over and talk to her. But what she doesn't know is that the man's mystery is not some strategy or way of picking up women,

it is his way of life. What neither of them know is that destiny will bring them together for an extra chance at being something special.

She decided that she needs a little extra help if she is going to truly study all night for her psych midterm tomorrow. So she goes into the coffee house for a little perk up before returning to the books. He simply decided that he couldn't sleep and decided to go for a walk. Is it a coincidence? Is it fate? She doesn't know, but she is going to find out, because she needs a little extra sugar.

"Hi. Could I have some sugar?"

He looks up very quickly. Either surprised by the fact that the woman he has admired for quite some time is actually talking to him, or because she asked for a kiss.

"I'm sorry?" he asks.

"Could I use the sugar that's in front of you? All the other ones are empty."

"Oh. Sure, go ahead."

She takes the sugar and pours it in her coffee, as if to give him more time to talk to her. It's amazing how he has all kinds of clever things to say to the men he has to get information from, but when it comes to her, he has no words. He finally comes up with something to say.

"For a second I thought you were asking something else."

"Oh really" she says snidely. "What exactly?"

"Um, well" he is trying to choose his words carefully, but since he has nothing catchy, he just goes with the truth. "I thought you were asking me to kiss you."

She seems somewhat taken aback by his honesty, yet also finds it refreshing.

"I haven't kissed someone I didn't know since the seventh grade."

"Really?" He says, very intrigued. "I bet there is a great story behind that statement."

"There is. But I only tell this story to people I know. Maybe if I knew your name I would tell you."

He hesitates, but after a brief and awkward silence, he finally answers.

"My name is Michael."

"I'm Grace."

"Please sit down Grace" says Michael. "You've drawn me in; I really want to hear this story. Why did you kiss someone you didn't know?"

"Well" Grace says as she sits down. "It was at a county Jr. High dance. My friends dared me to kiss the next boy to talk to me. Right after that, some boy bumped into me and said 'excuse me'."

Michael waits a little while for more.

"Is that it?"

"Yeah. Then I kissed him."

"Honestly that's a terrible story" he says through some laughter.

"Well excuse me. Most people like that story."

"Deaf people?"

Grace can't help but laugh, as does Michael.

"Ok Mr. Narrator, why don't you tell me one?"

"Wait a second, I didn't say I could do better, just that yours stunk."

"You talk a big game, now tell a big story."

"It's just that I do a lot of talking every day. You see my job requires me to sit in front of people and just ramble on until I get what

I want."

"What do you do?"

"I'm what I like to call an information getter."

Grace has no idea what that means, she doesn't even know what to ask in order to clarify.

"Any way," Michael says to quickly shift attention, "That's why I come here. I enjoy people watching. Seeing them enjoy each other's company, over hearing the loud ones."

"Staring at me" she interrupts.

"You cut right to the point. Don't you Grace?"

"I know. I know" she admits. "It's something I need to work on."

"No." He quickly says. "I really admire that in people."

Grace is surprised that Michael, or any guy for that matter, would feel that way.

"You see," Michael continues "People these days complain about how not enough gets done in this world, and that's it. They don't do anything about it. I admire those who actually back up what they say they're going to do. Especially you, because you seem like the kind of person who can do that just with words."

Grace is very impressed by that speech, to the point where she once again doesn't know how to respond. At least this time it's in a kind of awe for Michael. But something finally comes to her.

"Not a lot of people talk like that?"

"I guarantee you they feel that way. They just need people like you to say it first."

"That's sweet of you to say. But I don't know how brave I am. I'm stressing over these midterms."

"I'm pretty good at reading people. Trust me when I say this, you're brave enough to get through whatever life throws at you."

"Thanks for the pep talk" she says with sincerity. "I should get back to studying. I'll be done with my midterms on Friday. Maybe we can have dinner. You can finally tell me a story."

"Um, I don't usually go out with girls."

"Oh. I'm sorry, I didn't realize that you were…" she hesitates indicating that she has something very uncomfortable to say.

"Oh no." finally realizing what she means.

They both laugh out of embarrassment.

"I mean…What I'm trying to say is…" he stutters through the words.

While it appears that he can't seem to find the words to say, he does have the words. He just doesn't know which ones to use. Does he finally let someone into his life, or does he continue on with what he has grown to be content with: living through what he does for the cause of justice?

"I don't think that's a good idea. You see I never know when my phone will go off and where I'll be the next day."

"I'm willing to take a chance on you."

"But you see that's the thing. You don't know who I am. All you see is the quiet guy at the coffee house in the mornings that happen to be here tonight. But you don't know why I am here tonight. You don't know why I'm drinking Irish coffee instead of my usual, or anything else about me for that matter. So it's probably best for you that we just leave this as a nice encounter."

Grace sits there, as if to be stunned silent, but really she is staring at Michael with pity filled in her eyes.

"Well that seemed like a very nicely rehearsed speech. Does that work on all the people you want to push away?"

Michael doesn't know how to react to that.

"You said earlier that you were good at reading people, so am I. I was taught to only know what I see, but if I'm not sure, to theorize. You were right when you said I don't know you.

But I think I see a good man when I look at you." She begins to write on a napkin. "And I hope you see the same thing when you look in a mirror."

As Grace exits the coffee shop, Michael looks

at the napkin and it has her phone number on it. The ball is in his court. Right as he looks at it though, his phone rings. Watching Grace leave is very difficult for Michael. While he was completely honest with her, he is not sure if letting her leave was the right thing to do for him.

"Dear God, I dare not question your will. All I ask is for a clear sign of whether or not I should let that beautiful woman into my life while I pursue justice in your name. I ask this of you-"

Before he could finish his prayer a coffee house patron bumped into Michael, causing him to drop and break his phone. As if that wasn't enough of a sign, she also spilled her drink on it.

"Oh my God. I'm so sorry."

Michael doesn't need another sign to get the picture.

"You know what? That's fine. Here, have another coffee. And thank you."

He says as he dashes out of the coffee house hoping he gets a second chance with Grace.

Graces gets to her car, and takes a moment to stop and think about what just happened. At least she now has a name to go with the handsome man she has come to notice at the coffee shop.

"A penny for your thoughts" says Michael.

Grace jumps a little out of fear. Not because she's afraid of Michael, but more out of how spooky it is that she was just thinking of him.

"Sorry" says Michael. "Most of the time I do that without even trying."

"That's fine, but I thought we were done for the evening. I mean I did my whole speech with the dramatic exit and everything."

"Yeah" he says through a laugh. "You said you were taught to analyze, theorize and only know what you see. I was taught to believe in signs, which aren't always easy to see. But I was given a sign clear as day that tonight shouldn't end, at least on my account."

Grace can't figure out if Michael is serious with all this talk about signs or if this is some ploy to get her to bed, but regardless she is interested in seeing where this goes.

Perhaps it's her analytical mind that makes her intrigued at how Michael reveals a little at a time as opposed to most other guys that she can read like an open book. Or maybe it's simply that Michael is not put off by her straight shooting. Either way, there is an undeniable attraction.

"Tonight? I was going to use the last few hours of the night to study for my midterm" she says with a hint of regret.

"Trust me when I say this. If you don't turn off the work part of your brain every now and then, you will lose it all."

Even from what little interaction they have had, Grace can tell that Michael is sincere in what he says.

"Alright. What did you have in mind"

"Well it all depends on how much you trust me, and if you're up for a little bit of a walk."

Michael wasn't kidding when he said it was a bit of a walk. He's leading Grace through a forest with all kinds of twists and turns on the dirt path with nothing but his lantern.

"Look if you're going to kill and bury me, could you just do it now please?"

"We're almost there. I promise."

"Where is there?"

"One of the most beautiful sights in the world. Here we are."

Grace walks around a giant Redwood tree to see that Michael leads her to an outdoor chapel. While it looks fairly rustic with its wooden benches for worshipers to sit on and nothing but a dirt path leading to the altar, Michael wasn't kidding about one of the most beautiful sights ever. The chapel is on a hill top, and the stars are shining so bright that they barely need the lantern.

"Wow. What is this place?"

"My Mom used to take me here all the time. I come here when I need to turn off my brain."

"You think your Mom will mind coming here with someone other than her" Grace asks sarcastically.

"I don't think she'll mind."

Grace notices Michael had a little trouble saying that. She then notices a sign that reads 'Elizabeth Tetra Memorial Chapel.'

"I'm sorry Michael."

"It's fine. She brought me here when I was little. She taught me a very valuable lesson here."

"What's that?"

"Let me ask you this first? Do you go to church?"

"No. Not lately at least. I mean I believe that something is up there, but I just don't know what."

Michael laughs a little.

"Want to know a secret? That means you believe

in God. What you just described is what every religious person goes through. We don't know what is up there, no one does, but we believe that God is watching over us. Some people express that belief more than others, but a belief is nothing more than a hunch, no matter how strong it is."

"I guess I never thought of it like that. But like I said, I don't really go to church; I guess I'm not a very good believer."

"That doesn't matter. That's what my Mom

taught me. You see, one morning my parents had a big fight. They were so loud it woke me up. I couldn't hear what they were arguing about, but I could tell they were fighting. So my Mom came into my room, grabbed me out of bed and brought me here."

"Why here?"

"She wanted me to know that a church is just a place with four walls and people who say a bunch of memorized prayers. But God's presence is everywhere. Whether it's a hill top with a nice view, or just in the presence of someone nice. All we have to do is let him in our heart."

Grace smiles and stares at Michael with envy. How brave he is to share all that with someone whom he had just formally met that evening.

"So you mentioned that you're an 'information getter.' What does that entail that you would need to escape, to here?"

"Are you analyzing me?" he says with sweet concern. "I brought you here so you could avoid that."

"Forgive me, but it's who I am and what I love to do. I'm not sure I can turn it off."

"Oh well I guess we should just leave then" he says sarcastically.

"Hey you're not getting out of answering this question" she retorts.

"Jeez you'd make quite the information getter yourself."

"That's pretty much what I'm training to do when you think about it."

"Touché. Well there's not much to my job. People need information and I get it for them. Whether it's about a person, a product, or a location, whatever."

"Sounds like you're a private eye."

"Something like that yeah."

Grace is glad she finally got some kind of answer out of him; however, she does take notice of the remaining vagueness. But she is not going to let it ruin this wonderful time she is having with Michael.

"Sounds exciting."

"It can be. Not really when you compare it to the army though."

"Army huh? I can see that in you."

"Yeah. So did they. They thought I would be a career man, but it just got to the point where I needed something else. Oh hey, watch this."

Michael points out to the horizon where the sun is beginning to rise. The area where sunlight meets the dark sky is a beautiful sight to see.

"Wow it's like..."

Grace can't finish, but Michael knows exactly what she is thinking.

"Heaven?"

"Yeah. It's the most beautiful thing I've ever seen."

"Second most for me."

Grace can tell Michael means her when he says that. She rewards him for such a nice compliment with a kiss.

Michael is much happier returning to the garage this time than he was from his job. Never had he enjoyed someone's company more than the time he spent with Grace. As he goes to turn the light on, that feeling of happiness turns to suspicion when nothing happens.

"Father? Are you here?"

The light from the sun isn't much in the warehouse, but it's enough for Michael to see a man with a tire iron come at him. Michael ducks out of the way and is able to incapacitate him into an arm lock. Suddenly Michael sees that the assailant isn't alone when a man with a baseball bat comes at him. Michael is able to avoid that hit as well, but it's only a matter of time before the numbers game catches up to him.

Michael hits a hidden button that causes the windows to be completely covered. It is now pitch black and it doesn't matter how many men there are in the fight because no one can see anything.

"Where are you?" asks one of the assailants.

The two armed men can hear quick footsteps.

"Come out and fight" demands the other.

"Are you boys afraid of the dark?" asks Michael.

Every time the men think they know where Michael is, another quick set of footsteps runs by them.

"I'm not really afraid of it. I've just been in enough darkness to know that I prefer the contrary. I guess Job said it best: 'He redeemed my soul from going down to the pit, and I will live to enjoy the light.'

A strobe light is turned on. Though quick, it's bright enough to blind the armed assailants. Michael reveals himself, dressed in his interrogation outfit, the intruders are now facing the Masked Man. Michael shows that the army didn't just teach him how to gather information, but also how to defend himself. A kick to one of the men, a punch to the other. It also helps that they are on Michael's turf. He knows where to throw them, and what is available for him to use to make the intruders regret their decision. It doesn't take long for the men to be beaten into submission. Michael grabs the one that is still conscious.

"Why are you here?"

"Go to hell."

"Wrong answer" Michael says as he breaks a finger. The man screams in agony. "Next time the finger comes off. Now why are you here?"

The man still won't answer, so Michael stabs his hand through a table with "old reliable."

"You wait right here. I'll go get the sheers and cut that broken finger right off."

Michael gets five steps before the assailant has had enough.

"This is a test. We were let in here."

"What?" Michael asks as he stops in his tracks.

The lights turn on and the sound of clapping comes from above.

"Well done." Michael looks up to see a stranger standing on the scaffold with his father. "I always enjoy a good show."

"What is going on Father?"

"As my colleague just said, this was a test" the man says as he descends the stairs. "An audition if you will and you Michael passed with flying colors."

"I don't understand."

"Didn't your Father tell you that we were interested in procuring your services exclusively?"

"He talked about a meeting" he says with an angry stare at his Father, "But he didn't say with whom? Come to think of it, I still don't know who the hell you are?"

"Son" says Father.

"It's alright. I wouldn't like it either if a man I didn't know came into my house to judge me. My name is Seth Zern. Those are my associates Wyatt and Rome. I told them to come in and get you rattled up, but under no circumstances reveal anything. I like what I see in you Michael."

"Well Mr. Zern, I think it fair to warn you that I am only judged by one."

"Yes I could see that you're a man of faith. I liked the Job quote. I prefer 'Where the fear of God is wanting, there the country will come to ruin, unless it be sustained by the fear of the prince, which may temporarily supply the want of religion.'

"But as in the lives of princes, the kingdom will of necessity perish as the prince fails in virtue.' Machiavelli."

"Impressive" says Seth. "I guess I shouldn't be surprised that you know the words of the man whose philosophy was to embrace the bad as well as the good. You know those are two of the toughest men under my employ."

"Sorry to hear that."

Michael is not as impressed by Seth's intelligence or confidence as Seth is by Michael's skill set.

"We definitely want to go to the next level with you. Mr. Tetra." Father shakes his hand. "Michael." He extends his hand to Michael,

who doesn't return the courtesy. "We'll be

in touch."

Seth leaves with his cohorts close behind him, but not before Wyatt, the one who was stabbed in the hand, looks back at Michael with an ugly stare.

"What's the next level?" Michael quickly asks his Father.

"They want to see your work."

"My work isn't a damn sideshow. How could you agree to this? And how could you let them into our home?"

"I didn't know they wanted to test you like this. Michael, just keep the faith. Please.

We will continue dispensing justice; it'll

just be with their guidance."

Michael stares at his Father with disappointment and decides to leave before he says something he will regret.

CHAPTER 7

Michael has never been this nervous about a task before. He has fought battles, ran into buildings with bombs to save people, and is able to make the toughest men submit to his questioning. But nothing, not his military training or his everlasting faith can prepare him for his first official date with Grace.

He did do it right: A fancy restaurant complete with candle light and a band with a sultry singer. But as every smitten man knows, half the battle is keeping the conversation going. While Michael has no problem with small talk, in the back of his mind he knows that he can't divulge specifically what he does. He can't let her into his world. It is so ugly and scary, and she is so lovely.

"You look beautiful," says Michael.

"Thank you. I've always wanted to come here.

I thought you had to know somebody just to get on the three month wait list. Now I do."

"It's more like you know someone who knows someone who cashed in a favor or two just to beg to get me in here."

"Well regardless," she says as she raises her glass, "here is to a lovely evening."

"Here's to you having one last semester of school ahead of you." They toast but Grace has a less than excited look on her face. "Is something wrong?"

"I'm just not sure it'll be that simple."

"Come on. With your brains, I'm sure you'll get through the classes."

"It's not that. There's this T.A. in one of my classes. He keeps asking me out. I've tried to let him down gently but he is very persistent."

"He's not getting the message?"

"Worse than that, he's threatened to switch my grades with someone who is failing the class."

"That's terrible. Can't you go to the teacher?"

"That won't do much. His father is the professor."

"Oh great. What's his name?"

"Vernon Clive."

"Of course it is."

That gets Grace to smile. She absolutely lights up when the band begins to play Sinatra's 'Fly Me to the Moon.'

"I love this song."

"Then we better not waste it."

Michael leads Grace onto the dance floor. As good a fighter as he is, he is an even better dancer. Not only is Grace impressed by how light on Michael is on his feet, but she feels safe in his arms. Michael also gets that feeling from Grace. Not that he needs protection from anything, but rather he has a growing feeling of peace. When he's with Grace his mind isn't in the past where he relives the terrible things he went through. He is in the moment with Grace. As much fun as he had with Grace, something was bothering Michael that evening, more like someone. Vernon Clive.

It's not just about how much Michael cares for Grace; it's also a matter of how wrong what this guy is doing. If it's one thing Michael can't abide by, it's an abuse of power. Luckily Michael has just the solution.

The door step of Vernon's parents' house certainly wasn't the place Michael was hoping to be at the end of the night, but he'll take it.

"Try not to be too loud and wake up my parents" Vernon says to a young lady.

"Just make sure I get an A in the class and I'll be as quiet as you want" she says.

"I like the sound of that" Vernon says as he starts to sloppily kiss the young lady. "You see what I did there?"

"Yeah" she says with forced enthusiasm.

"Sound's good. It's funny because you'll be quiet for me."

Right on cue the masked man appears from out of nowhere.

"She gets it. She just doesn't give a shit."

"Hey-"

Vernon is cut off by the masked man grabbing him by the throat.

"Get lost," he says to the lady, who immediately does so.

"So. You like to get girls in bed by promising them good grades. Unless of course they already have good grades, then you black mail them. Does that sound right?" Vernon tries to talk but the grip around his throat is too tight. "What? I can't understand you. Oh I see."

He lets go and Vernon falls to his knees gasping for breath.

"Who are you?" Vernon says through the gasps.

"I'm Karma, and I'm here to catch up to you."

He picks Vernon up with ease since he's about as skinny as a pencil and slams him against the door.

"Please don't kill me," says Vernon.

"Shut up. I'm not going to kill you. I'm just going to beat the living shit out of you so you learn your lesson." Vernon starts to whence. "Don't worry I'll do it quietly so I don't wake up your parents."

"I promise I won't do this anymore. I won't trade higher grades for sex. I won't black mail girls to go out with me."

"That's very good Vernon" says the masked man as he picks Vernon up by scruffing his shirt.

"Wait" pleads Vernon. "What are you doing? I'm changing my ways so you won't beat me up."

"When did I agree to that?"

He cocks his fist back, but the masked man is only kidding. He knows he scared Vernon enough so he won't do it anymore. Still, as if to be saved by the bell, the masked man receives a text message. He looks at it and sees that Father lined up a job for him tonight.

"Lucky for you I have better things to do tonight. But don't make me come back here."

The masked man drops Vernon and disappears before he can even thank the masked man for sparing him.

It was supposed to be just another job like any other. Michael would get the task from his Father, become the masked man, and get the job done like always. But once again his Father surprises Michael with the appearance of Seth Zern and his associates.

"I don't like this" says Michael to his Father discreetly.

"This won't affect your work, my son. You're better at this than I am."

That compliment means a lot to Michael, but the fact that his Father said it to curve his resentment puts a damper on it.

"Michael, put these on" says Seth as he hands him a pair of what appear to be sun glasses. He has only said four words to Michael and Seth has already pissed him off.

"What are these?"

"The latest in recording technology. My company designed them."

"First of all, they're too big," says Michael, trying to insult Seth. "Second of all I only wear my mask. It's very important to me."

"You'll wear what we God damn tell you to wear" says Wyatt.

Michael stands up ready to go round two with Wyatt, but Seth steps in between them.

"Relax gentlemen. Michael would you be averse to wearing our recording shirt with the button cam? It's black."

Michael isn't alright with that either, but he knows how important this is to his Father, so he nods in agreement.

"Very good. Wyatt, go get it please."

Wyatt hasn't removed the angry stare since he got to the warehouse, even as he backs away to do as his boss tells him.

"You better keep your boy away from me" says Michael.

"He'll come around. You did mess up his hand you know" says Seth.

"He takes the Lord's name in my house again and his face is next."

"I like you Michael, I have a soft spot in my heart for my fellow Military brothers, but my company didn't become the top private security firm by letting people tell me what to do" says Seth with an obvious hint of threat.

Michael is torn between the utmost distrust of Seth Zern and the love and respect he has for his Father. He keeps trying to remember that his Father was an information getter just like him. He has already learned so much, he also has the opportunity to learn with him. Maybe teaming with Seth Zern can help further their cause.

"Military brothers huh? Where did you serve?"

"D.C." says Zern.

"Where?"

"I was one of the top advisers at the Pentagon."

And with that Michael is sorry he asked. One thing that is a certainty in all military is the hatred of pencil pushers who think they are soldiers, yet never even seen a battlefield.

"Here is the job son" says Father as he hands Michael the file he put together. "His name is Jordan Simon. Accused killer of Tracy Martinez."

"Accused?"

"I video chatted with the parents. They said their daughter and Jordan were dating."

"It says here he's 30 and she was 17."

"That's right. Jordan was the prime suspect. He claimed that Tracy wanted to do it on the beach with him, but he said no and she was so upset she stormed off and left him. They found her body about a mile down the shore where she left him, strangled to death."

"But he was found innocent?"

"No, it was a mistrial. Some rookie Medical Examiner botched the report before Simon was even put on the stand to testify. The parents just want to hear him confess to it."

Michael nods in agreement, letting the anger build inside him. It comes with the job that he has to make himself angry at the man he is going to get information from before he even meets him.

"What are you going to do to him?" asks Seth.

"Whatever I have to do" says Michael. "Where are they keeping him?" he asks his Father.

"That's the catch," says Father. "This all happened in New York. According to the Martinez family he left about a week ago and has family in San Francisco. They've been following him on one of those damn social websites. He seems to spend many nights at a bar in the Presidio. They're paying us extra for our efforts."

"How do we get him?"

"Leave that to us" says Seth.

Michael's Father gives him a look that says I told you so. As much as Michael hates to admit it, knowing Seth Zern is paying off. In less than an hour Seth and his associates had Jordan Simon in their storage container.

It's like a scene out of a low budget horror movie for Jordan Simon. He's tied to a chair with duct tape over his mouth, one lamp hooked up to a car battery, and a masked man with a bag of tricks. Jordan tries to scream but the tape makes it impossible for him to be heard. The masked man sets up an audio recorder to send to the Martinez family.

"Confession is good for the soul. I guarantee you it will be good for your health" says the masked man as he rips off the duct tape.

"What is this?" asks Jordan.

"This is an opportunity for you to receive mercy for what you did to Tracy Martinez."

"But I was found innocent."

"Hey" he says as he slaps the taste out of Jordan's mouth. "Do not lie. You got off on a technicality. There's a big difference between innocent and not guilty. Which are you?"

"You got a lot of nerve talking about innocence. Is this acceptable where you come from?"

The masked man gets right in Jordan's face.

"You can turn this around on me all you want. But this situation right now is about you and what the Martinez family wants."

"I didn't do anything to Tracy. I loved her."

"I said don't lie. And now you will be punished."

Jordan flinches in fright, but all that happens is the masked man turns on his I-pod to play 'Last Friday Night' by Katy Perry. Jordan is perplexed by the masked man's song choice.

"You're punishing me with a song?" asks Jordan with hesitation.

"Why would this song be a punishment? I thought you, of all people, would like this song. It talks about better times from before, nice memories that we can relive again. Isn't that why you dated Tracy in the first place? To relive your youth?"

"I'm only 26. I don't need to relive anything."

"You're 30, jackass." says the masked man as he sidekicks Jordan. "See? You can't help but lie. Jordan this is a win-win. I know you think you won the freaking lottery with a mistrial. But if you continue this lie for the rest of your life, you will live it in sin, perish into the eternal flames of Hell. Until you say aloud what you've done, you can't begin your path of inner peace, and two parents can't begin their healing."

Jordan takes a deep breath.

"They never accepted mine and Tracy's relationship. So fuck their healing, and fuck you to."

"Oh Jordan. I was afraid you would say something that stupid."

The masked man round house kicks Jordan and down he goes. He then cranks up the music even louder and begins to pummel Jordan. Just punch after punch all over the place. He can't hit Jordan too hard in the face since he needs the words to clearly come out of his mouth. After a minute he finally stops and props Jordan back up and puts a pause on the recorder.

"Listen Jordan, Tracy's parents think they

know. I'm sure the Prosecutor, the police, and probably every juror thought they knew as well. But me, I know."

"Why are you doing this to me?" The masked man has a vision of a teenage boy screaming that. "Please no more." says Jordan and the masked man has another vision, this time of a man screaming that. "How could you possibly know that I am guilty?" Jordan says through some deep breaths.

The masked man composes himself back to reality.

"Because, unfortunately, I can see the darkness inside everyone. That is why I am able to do this. I can get whatever I want from someone in your position because I know when they are lying and, more often than not, I find out why. It's just a matter of time and pushing the right button."

He goes over and turns the recorder back on and crouches down to the same level of Jordan who has had enough.

"I killed Tracy. We were on the beach and she was just so beautiful." The masked man smacks Jordan in the head as a subtle reminder to keep it about the confession.

"She started talking about taking our relationship to the next level but I told her I wasn't ready and people probably wouldn't accept us."

Jordan begins to tear up.

"Keep going" says the masked man as he has another vision of a man saying that.

"We started arguing and she started yelling at me. I was afraid someone would call the police. So I grabbed her and dragged her under the pier so we could talk privately and when I let go she was dead. I killed her, but I swear it was an accident."

Jordan is now crying. By now 'Last Friday Night Ended' and 'Teenage Love Affair' by Alicia Keys had begun. The masked man is very good at reading people, and he can tell that Jordan is legitimately upset for what he did. He turns off the recorder and the music.

"Jordan, do you know what a baptism of fire is?" Jordan nods no. "It's when someone goes through a terrible and somehow painful ordeal, but comes out of it stronger. So this can either be you getting beaten down, or this can be your baptism of fire. That is up to you. I'm sorry for what you must be going through knowing that you killed someone, but you have been granted a second chance. Take it."

Jordan doesn't have words. He watches the masked man leave and shut the container door behind him.

Michael is met outside by Seth Zern who appears to be pleased.

"If you'll be with us, welcome to Chaos Security."

Seth extends his hand again, and this time Michael shakes it and takes off the camera shirt.

"Can you get him back to his hotel?"

"Of course. Oh I was wondering, there was a moment where it looked like you kind of lost your shit. What was that?"

"Just get him out of here." Michael says as he walks away. Seth proved himself useful, but he doesn't owe him an explanation. Plus, he has to close out with his usual ritual. "Dear God, I believe you sent that man to me to put him on the path. I now leave it in your hands. Please guide him to the destination of righteousness. May my life be an example of your justice.
I ask these of you, and in your son's name I pray. Amen."

"Keep going" says a man in military camouflage.

"Please no more" says another man.

A vision of a teenage boy screaming through a gag causes Michael to finally wake up from his flashback. As usual he is breathing hard and sweating. But at least this time he isn't alone since he is in Grace's bed.

"Hey. Are you okay baby?" says Grace.

"Yeah. I'm fine."

Michael kisses Grace to reassure her, but she knows he is lying. This isn't the first time Michael has woken up this way, but she doesn't understand why he just keeps insisting that 'he's fine.' Why does he go through this burden alone? She really wants to find out so he can feel as safe around her as she does with him. Michael immediately falls back asleep, so maybe he already does. But she still wants to help him.

There was a time for Michael when he enjoyed mornings. Seeing it as a potential fresh start, going from darkness to light. Unfortunately he lost that feeling after the military, but since he started staying with Grace, that feeling has come back. Hopefully he can keep it.

"Good morning" says Grace as she puts out breakfast for them.

"Good morning. Sorry about waking you last night."

"It's alright. Do you want to talk about it?"

"No. It's no big deal."

Michael begins to eat in order to divert attention, but Grace isn't satisfied with that answer.

"Babe, I think you should talk about it. You wake up in the middle of the night screaming from your nightmare. It sounds like PTSD."

"You just asked if I wanted to talk. I don't want to or need to. Besides, you wouldn't understand."

"You're probably right. But I know some people who would. There's a group of veterans who meet at my school. It's open to veterans, family members, anyone really. Maybe they can help you."

"I don't need help. I know how to get through this."

"How?"

"Penance." Grace just stares at Michael. "See I knew you wouldn't understand."

"You're right I don't. Is this some Catholic guilt thing?"

"My father went through exactly what I'm going through. He survived by making up for it. Not by sitting in a circle and singing Kumbaya while crying." Michael notices that Grace is looking off to the side. "What? I know when you're thinking about something. "

"It sounds like classic denial with a subconscious urge to please your Father while self-inflicting guilt-"

"Oh God" he snaps to interrupt Grace's diagnosis. "Keep your damn analysis to yourself and don't try to understand things you never will."

With that Michael storms out. Grace isn't sad or angry with Michael, but she is definitely disappointed. She just wants Michael to feel better and to know that what he is going through, he doesn't have to bear it alone. Michael isn't really angry with Grace either, but he meant that there is no way Grace will understand what he goes through, or even worse that maybe she will. Regardless Michael would have to leave anyway because Father lined up another job.

The second Michael walked into the warehouse Father knew something was off. Even more so than after he gathered information from John Locke.

"Where were you?" asked Father.

"Out having breakfast. What's the job?"

"His name is Nickolas Gregg. His ex-wife hired us."

"What does she want?"

"Her dog."

"Come again?" asks Michael because he really can't believe how low his job has sunk. "I'm not a repo-man."

"Her ex got custody of their pure bread or something or other in the divorce. She's offering ten grand for it."

"Rich people" says Michael with disgust. "Fine, where do I find him?"

"She said he goes for a run every night at the beach. Sometimes with the dog, sometimes without."

"The beach?"

"Yeah. Is that okay?"

"Sure. I'll call you when I'm done."

"What's the rush? He doesn't run until night."

"Oh right."

"What's with you? What are you not telling me?"

"Jesus Christ I wish everybody would stop looking for what's not there."

"Hey" Father says as he hits Michael in the head. "You know we don't take Lord's name in vain."

Michael didn't even realize he said it.

"Maybe we shouldn't take the job," says Michael.

"We already accepted it. Besides, we never turn our back on dispensing God's justice."

"What if some rich bitch her dog back?"

"Do not judge by appearances, but with right judgment. John 7:24. For all we know this dog is the most important thing in this woman's life. Get your head in the game. You can't have moments of weakness when we start working for Zern."

"Impressing Zern is way down on my priority list. Besides, it's been months since we agreed to work with him. What the hell is he waiting for? I do this because you told me it is the path of penance and the way of justice."

"It is. But there are certain realities we have to face. We need money to survive and we need people to spread the word. So I suggest you take the time to grow up and realize that."

Father leaves Michael with that to think about. He was right about one thing, Michael is off his game. It's like he has reached full capacity in how much emotion he can hold in his heart. Regardless, the job must be done.

It's unfortunate that where Michael goes to soothe his soul is now the scene of his next interrogation. He almost feels sorry for Nickolas Gregg. Maybe this is also his place to unwind, but it's about to become his own personal nightmare.

The head light is enough for Nick to see the ground in front of him, but not enough to see someone come from out of nowhere and sweep his leg. The fall was more scary than painful, but it soon became nothing compared to the sight of looking up at the masked man.

"Please don't hurt me" begged Nick. "I don't have any money."

"I'm really not in the mood to fucking deal with this right now."

"Here, this watch is very expensive. Take it please."

"I'm not here for money" says the masked man as he slaps the watch away. "I'm here to tell you to let go."

"I don't understand."

"Let your ex-wife have the dog."

"That's what this is about? But I don't want to give up Rex."

The masked man steps on Nick's back to make sure he knows how serious he is.

"This isn't about what you want. Your ex wants the dog, so much so, she asked me to get it from you. The court can't help you, that dog can't help you; no one can help you so just give up the damn dog now."

He looks down and sees the sheer look of terror in Nick's eyes. This is usually where he flashes back, but instead he looks over at the lifeguard tower and sees himself with Grace on a recent date they had, her in his arms watching the waves crash against the shore. He decides to take a different approach with Nick instead of beating what he wants out of him and takes his foot off him.

"Look" says the masked man in a softer tone. "It looks like you both care about the dog. Can't you and your ex work something out?"

Nick is hesitant to answer in case this niceness is a set up. But he decides to sit up and talk to the masked man.

"No, she can have the dog. I like the dog but I was being selfish."

"What do you mean?"

"She loves that dog more than I do. I just wanted it because it was a nice reminder of what I used to have. Before me and her got so angry with each other. Pretty stupid huh?"

The masked man can relate to Nick. It's not to the same extent, but they are both two men stuck in the past."

"That actually makes more sense than you think.

Look I don't know how great it was with your ex before now, but take my advice, give her the dog, and go make new memories."

"That's it? That's all you're going to do to me?" Nick stupidly asks.

"Go" screams the masked man.

Nick gets up and starts running. The masked man begins to soak in the sounds of the waves as it is once again the place for him to soothe his soul. But that's not the only sound he hears. He also hears a loud "Thank you" from Nick as he runs away. That is definitely a first for the masked man. He looks up to the sky, and instead of his usual prayer he nods in agreement. He knows that God sent this man to him, not in the name of justice, but so that Michael can learn from it.

CHAPTER 11

"Welcome everyone." says Grant Klein, a typical looking young war veteran who you wouldn't want to meet in a dark alley. "Let's begin today with the introduction of a newcomer. What is your name and a little about yourself?"

"My name is Michael. I served in the army for two tours, mostly in Afghanistan and other places I'm not allowed to say."

The circle of veterans and family members of the support group Grace suggested to Michael welcome him with 'hellos' and waves.

"Thank you for your service Michael" says Klein. "I'm sure Michael is here for the same reason all of us are here. We feel alone. No one can understand what we went through, what we saw in Europe or Asia or in the Middle East. No one except those of us here. It doesn't matter where or when, war is war, it's harsh, it's ugly, but the worst part is its scarring, it's eternal." These are all the things that Michael has thought about, all the words he had used in his own thoughts and prayers. "So we start the meetings with those who want to share their progress in getting better. Who would like to begin? Bart?"

"Sure." says Bart Weston, a two time war veteran and retired career man. Old enough to have served in World War 2 and Korea and big enough to be his own platoon. "Well as you can all imagine I've been around long enough to see everything."

"Serving in the army will do that to you." says Grant.

"No, not because of the army. I mean, I got to see the world and do some incredible things thanks to the army, but when I met my Amy was when I saw everything because she was my one."

The older veterans nod in agreement while the younger ones, Michael included, are confused by Bart's statement.

"I can see you youngsters don't quite know what I mean" continues Bart. "When I fought in WW2 I was an orphan and single young punk. I didn't care if I lived or died. When I got back from the fighting was when I met Amy, and suddenly she was the one thing I had in my life that kept me going. When I was in a fox hole, shooting my gun, walking miles in blazing heat with a full pack, it was her face I saw. I lost her to cancer three years ago" Bart says as he begins to choke up. "I was either staring at the bottom of a bottle or down the barrel of a gun. That was it, nothing else to live for. Then Grant found me in a bar and told me about this group. Amy once again became my one. I want to tell everyone about her so maybe you kids won't go further than I did."

The group applauds Grant for his progress.

"Many people think life in the army is different from life outside of it" Grant interjects. "That's not the case for us. The war doesn't really end; the battle isn't won, because what we see and go through stays with us forever. That's why we all need that one in our lives. Maybe it's an "Amy", maybe it's faith and sobriety, or maybe it's family. But please know that you are not alone. We will help you find that one."

After his first meeting Michael suddenly doesn't feel so bad about what he is going through. While some men are talking about struggling to find his one, he has three of them. He's lucky that he found Grace, also that he has such a strong faith, and even though they don't see eye to eye at the moment, he still has his father.

"This is a nice thing you do here, Grant," says Michael.

"Thanks. I just wish I could do more."

"What do you mean?"

"Well sometimes I know taking these guys to their respective war memorials would help in the healing, or if I could get my hands on some better materials, but we can't afford it."

"You don't get funding?"

"The VA program in the university gives what it can but it's not much after paying for transportation, outside help, helping the families with small bills. I just do what I can."

"I hope you can keep going."

"So do I. I noticed you didn't have much to say. Saving it all for next time?"

"We'll see. Thanks a lot Grant."

"Hope to see you again brother."

Michael enjoyed talking to Grant, but he had somewhere he wanted to be. This was about the time Grace's night class ended and Michael, now more than ever, knew what he wanted to do. He got there with enough time to catch Grace coming out of her class. Even though they were apart for a short time he missed her so much.

"Hey" says Michael. How are you?"

"I'm fine. What are you doing here?"

"I went to the meeting."

"That's great. How do you feel?"

"A lot better than before. You were right."

"I'm just glad you found some people to talk to."

"The thing is I realized that I already did. You."

"Want to get out of here? Go back to my place?"

"Absolutely" says Michael without hesitation.

They walk off hand in hand; glad to be in each other's company again. But Michael's smile slowly fades away when he sees the local paper. The head line reads 'Body of Murder Suspect from New York Found.'

CHAPTER 12

"What is it?" asks Grace the second they sit down on her bed.

"Don't worry about it. Let's not ruin this night."

"No you're not doing that again. I saw the change. Please tell me what it is?"

"Grace I've seen and done things that I'm not proud of. I don't want you to have those images in your head. And I don't want you to see me differently."

"I love you" says Grace with tears in her eyes. "Please let me in and maybe I can help you."

Michael believes Grace loves him, because he loves her too. He has come so far in his emotional and spiritual healing; maybe he can go even further if he tells her what sent him down this path of information getting. The down side to sharing means that he is going to relive it, so vividly that it's like he is there.

"I was in the middle of my second tour of duty, serving with a special team of gorilla soldiers. We're the kind of soldiers that don't get to be on CNN or Good Morning America and nobody video tapes our surprise homecomings. To join this company you need to live by the code of finishing the task no matter what." Michael can see himself and his comrades getting ready for battle.

"We were led by a man named Colonel Hartley.

Everyone called him 'Hartless' because there were all kinds of rumors of terrible missions he was on. I guess I just hoped they weren't true."

Michael struggles to say more.

"It's okay. Let it out." says Grace to comfort him.

"Like I said, I'm an information getter. My job is to torture people until I get what I want. It didn't bother me because they were soldiers like me. I thought this was how I could best serve my country, just like my Father did before me. Hartley came to me with an assignment, they found out where one of the higher ups of Al-Qaida lived. My task was to find out the location of a weapon cache that if we got a hold of would have crippled their arsenal supply. Just another day in the office for me. We infiltrated his house no problem, but when I went into the room he wasn't tied to a chair. Instead, it was a kid."

"What?"

Michael is now having a full-on flashback. It's as if he is in Afghanistan with his outfit talking to Hartley. Michael enters the room, but not exactly as the masked man. Instead, he is wearing a crude sort of mask with simple welding goggles and a black scarf covering his mouth, as are his comrades in the group. Whether it is unity or fear, the mask and scarf are doing their job.

"There is no sense in torturing him," says Hartley. "He made a death pact with his fellow mop heads. But he has one weakness for sure, family. He won't hold on while he and his wife watch their son get tortured."

"This isn't what I signed on for," says Michael.

"You vowed to protect America from any and all threats. How many of your fellow soldiers will be killed by that weapon cache if we don't get to it first?"

As much as it pains Michael he can't disagree with Hartley's logic. Michael becomes the masked man, walks up to the teenager tied in the chair and begins to rough him up with a few well-placed punches. The parents scream while watching their worst nightmare happen in front of them.

"Mr. Jumbari," says Hartley. "I know you are a very educated man. You have a nice position with Al-Qaida; you can speak our language, and have acquired a small fortune because of these things. Now I need you to use that education to come up with a location that will put an end to what you see before you. Otherwise, my associate will continue to do what he does best."

Hartley nods at Michael who empties his bag filled with tools of the trade.

"I don't know what you're talking about," says Mr. Jumbari.

"That's unfortunate" says Hartley as he looks at Michael.

Michael gets a noose and wraps it around the boy's neck and lifts him off the ground, chair and all.

"Why are you doing this?" screams Mrs. Jumbari.

"Calm your wife Mr. Jumbari. Soldier, put him down."

Michael lets go of the rope to let the kid fall down, which causes the gag to fall off. Michael props the kid, who decides to speak, back up.

"Why are you doing this to me?" the boy asks. Michael quickly puts the gag back on.

"Please" says Mr. Jumbari. "Just tell me what you want to know and I will tell you."

"Don't play games with us or my associate will inflict more harm on your son."

"This is not a game" screams Mr. Jumbari. "I don't know what you're talking about."

"Maybe this will help you." says Hartley, which is the cue for Michael to get the taser. He sets it at its lowest voltage, and applies it to the boy's neck. "What are you his babysitter? Up the voltage soldier."

Michael hesitates, but turns it up and applies it again, and watches the boy convulse. The air is filled with the screams of the Mother and scent of the boy's urine.

"Uh latitude seventy-two degrees, longitude eighty-four degrees" says Mr. Jumbari.

Michael pulls away the taser, relieved that the father said something. But that relief goes away when Hartley begins to laugh an evil chuckle.

"Nice try Mr. Jumbari. Revealing the location of an abandoned house of one of your higher ups is clever. Unfortunately, for you, Uncle Sam already found and claimed that house as his own. Something tells me you already knew that though. I guess you're just not taking us seriously. Soldier, use this on the boy."

Hartley extends his hand holding a dagger for Michael to use.

"I don't need that," says Michael. "I got my own tools."

"Your tools aren't working. Once you stick this in that boy, his father will give in."

"Are you sure he knows something?"

"Do not question me, soldier." Michael looks to his comrades for support, but they are as lethal as Hartley. "That is a direct order."

Michael reluctantly takes the dagger and walks up to the boy. His fist is clenched so tight as if he's trying to make the dagger crumble in his hands. He cocks his arm back, but can't follow through.

"Fine I'll do it" says Hartley. "I just hope I don't cut too far."

"Wait" says Michael. He takes a deep breath and

sticks the dagger in the boy's leg. The boy writhes in pain but has no voice left to scream.

"There is only one step after this Mr. Jumbari. You know it and I know it. Give me the location."

Jumbari takes a moment to think and then motions to a door. Hartley picks him up and makes him go through the door, which leads to an office, leaving Mrs. Jumbari alone with the soldiers. She keeps an angry stare on Michael who tries not to look her in the eyes, but he can't help it.

"What kind of a man are you?" she screams at Michael who can't give her an answer.

Hartley emerges from the room with a file in hand.

"Mission accomplished boys" says Hartley. Michael takes the dagger out of the boy's leg and looks him over.

"He needs a doctor," says Michael.

"Then they better get him to one," says Hartley. "Jumbari tripped a silent alarm in the office. We have to go. Besides, being passed out is the best medicine for that kid after what you did to him."

Hartley motions and the team exits. Michael looks back at the Jumbaris as he leaves. The ride back to the base is like a fog for Michael. The next thing he knows he is on his knees saying his prayer for forgiveness.

"Do yourself a favor Michael," says Hartley, "forget about that kid. You did what was right by us."

"No. I did what was right by my country. I'll feel better when we get our hands on that weapon cache."

"Relax. We'll leave tomorrow at dawn. Good work."

Hartley steps outside for a victory cigar like he's Hannibal from the A-Team. The anticipation is making Michael antsy. He knows that if he just looks at the location of the weapon cache he'll begin to feel better. He picks up the file folder and looks at the papers inside, but he doesn't feel better. He quickly goes from nervous, to confused, and then to angry. He storms outside for answers.

"What the fuck is this?" asks Michael as he throws the file folder in front of Hartley. "This isn't a weapons cache. It's just the location of some oil well."

"Not just some oil well, the biggest one in the

country. I know some people in DC that will pay top dollar for the location of a well like this. Couldn't have done it without you Michael. We'll all make some nice scratch thanks to you."

"You son of a bitch you lied to me."

"Aw. Poor naive Michael. Knew what kind of a man he signed up to work with and was still expecting us to just hold hands and pick flowers."

"What about serving your country? Helping your soldier brothers? Or was that all bull shit?"

"You're damn right it is. I've been in this man's army for a long time. Here is something I like to teach the young men under my control: this army, this country, hell this world is about making money now in the present. It's about getting what you can as fast as you can and not giving a flying fuck about the rest."

"I don't believe that."

"Ha, of course you don't. A God damn altar boy. I can respect if you believe in Heaven and Hell, but if that is the case, you think saying some kind of apology to your precious God means we don't have a one-way ticket to the devil's back yard? In the words of the Grateful Dead: at least I'm enjoying the ride."

Michael picks up the file and throws it in the fire.

"You won't get to do this ever again."

"You think I don't already have a copy?" says Hartley.

"How about I send you to Hell sooner rather than later?" says Michael as he takes out his switch blade knife.

"What do you think of that, boys?"

Michael looks around and sees that his fellow soldiers have surrounded him and appears to share the same sentiment with Colonel Hartley.

"Besides Michael," says Hartley as the others put on welding goggles, "you want us to find that oil well. You don't want that boy to have died for nothing do you?"

"Died?" asks Michael.

"Keep practicing, maybe someday you'll get the information you want without killing some poor boy to get it."

One of the soldiers throws a flash bang grenade. Michael goes to grab his goggles, but realizes he doesn't have them. In a last stitch effort to do something Michael lunges at Hartley as the grenade goes off.

The flash of light brings Michael back to the present where he is in Grace's bedroom. He screams as if he is attacking Hartley all over again, but Grace is there to calm him down.

"Michael, look at me," says Grace. "You're here with me. Not with that evil man, not in that terrible place. You're here with me."

Michael looks around, unsure of how he went from Afghanistan to Grace's bedroom. This was the first time Michael relived the whole experience from beginning to end.

"I'm sorry babe."

"It's fine. What happened next?"

"When I regained my eye sight all I saw were my knife with blood on it and the MP's arresting me. I never saw Hartley again."

"Why did they arrest you?"

"I was charged with desertion, and then dishonorably discharged. So, I came back home. My father convinced me that the best way to get through this was to perform penance. To do the sins that others won't in the name of justice."

Grace is stunned by what Michael went through. While she is glad he shared it with her, she now finds herself unsure of what to do now.

"Michael, I should apologize to you."

"Why?"

"Because, even with all my training I don't know how to help you. I can't even begin to imagine what you're feeling right now."

Michael stares at Grace with a smile because there is a way she can help him. He lies down in her arms and she holds him as he begins to fall asleep.

CHAPTER 13

Things could not be better for Michael. He has not, nor has he even felt the urge, to become the masked man for weeks. Between his time with Grace and going to the weekly meetings his mind, body, and soul are the closest he has ever been to having inner peace. This week he is combining the best of both worlds because he asked Grace to go with him to the next meeting. As if to be a test directly from God Michael's phone goes off with a call from Father right as he and Grace are walking into the class room. Grace has a brief feeling of concern, but that goes away quickly when Michael shuts his phone off without hesitation.

"The things we saw and did while we served wouldn't be so bad if it just happened to us," says Michael to the group, "but as with most evil things there are innocent bystanders. We often ask why we survived when all our buddies we served with didn't get to, we can't help but wonder if the suicide bomber really wanted to do that job, or why do the kids playing in the streets catch the stray bullets?" Grace can tell it's hard for Michael to share, so she holds his hand for support. "There's a phrase that I'm sure all the veterans have heard before; I've seen the elephant. This means for better or worse we've seen it all. I agreed with what Grant said at the first meeting I came to, serving in the army is scarring. Whether it was because of what we saw, what he had to do, or what we chose to do. One thing I was taught as an information getter was to be in the moment with the person you are getting information from, but not stay there in that moment. I couldn't do that. I would look to the past for answers that weren't there.

Well I've decided that if I am going to be stuck in a moment it's only going to be, God willing, in a moment with those I love."

The group gives applause to Michael who gets a supportive kiss from Grace.

"That's great to hear Michael" says Grant. "Along those lines I would like to give everyone these. They are healing journals designed specifically for veterans. You can write about your progress; you can detail your fractured flashbacks."

"Where did you get these?" asks Bart.

"I found a satchel of cash left for the program in my office a few weeks back. Now I can give you guys the materials we deserve."

"If I found that satchel, I'd be in Vegas by now" which gets a laugh from the room. Who donated the money?" asks Bart.

"Didn't say. I just found a note with it that said 'keep going.' And that's what we'll all get to do in our healing. Great meeting everyone. Hope to see you next week."

Grace smiles at Michael because she knows it was him that left the cash donation. Michael just smiles back and winks. They leave the meeting and stop at a diner.

"Michael, are you happy with how things are right now?" asks Grace.

"Grace, I'm the happiest I've been in a long time. Why?"

"I have to ask you something and I want to know that this is really you being happy. That you're not just putting on a brave face for me."

"What do you want to ask me?" Michael can see Grace hesitating and struggling to find the words. "Babe, you can ask me anything. You helped me get through one of the hardest things in my life. There is nothing that can come between us."

"I've been offered a job doing family counseling. It's in Chicago."

"Chicago? Well I guess there are a lot of families there. I'm sure some of them could use counseling" Michael says as a pathetic attempt to hide the tension he feels for possibly losing Grace.

"I want you to come with me," says Grace. "I can do what I love and you can have a completely new start. We can have a new start."

Michael is unsure of what to say. While he is glad of the progress he has made towards inner peace, the thought of him completely giving up what he does has never crossed his mind before.

"Wow. Chicago huh?" says Michael as another failed attempt at a brave face.

"Look, don't answer right now. I know it's a lot to take in, especially with all that's been going on, but I love you Michael and I want to be with you."

"I love you too. I just need to process everything right now."

"That's fine" says Grace. "I have to use the bathroom. I'll be right back."

As Grace leaves Michael holds her hand as long as he possibly can and watches her all the way out of sight. Michael turns back and sees the last thing he expected, Father entering the diner.

"Father. What are you doing here?"

"I saw your car in the parking lot. Why didn't you answer your phone?"

"I turned it off and forgot to turn it on," he says quickly. "Look, now is not a good time. I'll talk to you back at the house."

Michael tries to guide Father out the door and notices a blood stain on his shirt.

"What's the rush? Oh, I get it you're here with that girl. Are you suddenly ashamed of me?"

"First of all her name is Grace, second you're not exactly dressed for the occasion" indicating the blood stain on Father's shirt.

"Michael, who's this?" asks Grace.

Michael quickly zips up Father's jacket to cover the stain.

"You must be Grace" says Father. "I have been waiting to meet you for a long time."

"Grace," says Michael as if he is surrendering, "this is my Father."

"Oh." says Grace, taken by surprise as much as Michael was. "It's nice to meet you."

"Like wise" says Father. "Sorry I can't stay. I'm on my way back from a long day of work."

"I can imagine" says Grace out of reflex. She wishes she could take it back, hoping she didn't reveal that she knows what they do."

"Yes, well, you two have a lovely night" says Father as he exits the diner.

Michael and Grace share a look of concern. Michael knows his evening just got a lot longer and difficult.

Michael enters the warehouse looking for Father. He finds him in his bedroom removing his shirt, seeing that it had more blood on it than he realized.

"Welcome home Michael," says Father. "Assuming this still is your home."

"Stop it Father. What's with the blood?"

"Like I said, you didn't answer your phone. Seth had a job for us. Someone had to do it."

"Zern? I told you we weren't going to do business with that murderer."

"Oh give it a rest Michael. So they got rid of the guy by killing him. He was a kiddy diddler. Maybe this was the best way to get rid of him."

"That is not for us to decide. We don't kill. We let God handle that part. That is what you taught me."

"Things change Michael. We adapt, or parish."

"I'm the one doing his work. I'm the one out there putting myself through Hell, doing everyone's sins, not you. So if I don't want to work for Zern, I won't" Michael screams.

Father and Michael just stare at each other for a minute.

"Fine," says Father. "He's out. You win."

"I'm not trying to win, Father. What we do is hard enough without having to worry about trusting Zern."

"You mean since you met Grace?"

"Yes" says Michael without hesitation. "I just don't know if I want to do this anymore. If I gather information with doubt then things will go bad and you know it."

"And that group you go to will help you get over what you did in the army?" Michael is stunned silent. He knows father is good, but can't comprehend how he knows about the group. "I guess we're both facing some doubt right now."

"Do you always follow me?" asks Michael.

"I'm a Father watching over his son. Are you going to hold that against me?"

"Father. I'm done."

Michael tries to end the conversation by walking away.

"So what now? Get a regular job, get a house you can't afford with Grace, have kids and try to live a normal life."

"Why not? You did."

"And look what happened Michael." says Father with an outburst. Father sits down, breathing hard, almost overcome with grief. Michael joins him. "God won't stop throwing things in your way. I don't want you to learn that when it is too late."

"Father, I lost her too. I understand that things rarely happen the way you plan it."

"I have cancer Michael." interrupts Father.

"What?"

"The doctors have given me a couple years at the most."

"There has to be something we can do. A specialist you can see. We've got money."

"I've seen them all, son."

"Why didn't you tell me?"

"My job of protecting you is never done. But I need your help now. Please help me cleanse my soul before God takes me. Only a lifetime of penance will ensure our place in heaven."

Michael stares at the ground like he can see through it. He can't turn his back on the one who gave him life when he needs him the most, which means he has to return to what puts him through emotional Hell, and in order to do that, he has to do something he doesn't think he'll be able to come back from.

"Grace" says Michael on the phone "can I come over?"

Michael is unsure of which will be more difficult to do: reliving the flash back, or having this conversation with Grace. How does he tell the one that has helped him get through a difficult time, who was the source of his inner healing, that he is going back to what he does?

"Hey come on" says Grace. "Remember what you said to me? That I can tell you anything. It goes both ways." Like the first time they met Michael can't seem to find the words. "I'm sorry if I made things weird between you and your Father. I didn't mean to let on that I know. I wanted you to be able to tell him that when you were ready to."

"Grace" says Michael, mainly to get her to stop talking and making what he has to say even harder to do so. "I can't stop."

"What do you mean? Can't stop what?"

"My Father told me about some jobs lined up, and I'm going to do them."

"Why? How can you go back to that way of life?"

"I can't help it. It's who I am. It's what I was put here to do. For what I have done, and what I have failed to do, I must devote my life to this cause of justice."

"That's your father talking to Michael. You sound like a damn drone. Don't listen to him."

"Don't you get it?" screams Michael. "He knows me better than you. He knows this is what I have to do in life. What did you think was going to happen? I would settle down with you? Ride off into the sunset to Chicago. I couldn't live a life like that. Not after what I've seen. So do yourself a favor and just move on."

"Stop it. If you don't want to be with me, then at least be honest. It's because you're still letting someone else get in the way of your happiness. Of living your life. First you did it in the army, and you're doing it now with your father."

"Shut up. Stop acting like you understand me. If you did then you would have listened to me when we met at the cafe and I said let's leave this as a nice encounter. But like an idiot I chased after you, and got sidetracked from what my life is all about. Have a nice life in Chicago."

Michael storms out because he knows he can't take anymore of hurting Grace, but he knows it is what must happen in order to protect her from the world he can't fully escape from. Michael's mind goes from clear to being in a fog. The next thing he knows he is inside his room tearing it apart by punching holes in his wall, throwing pictures and ripping apart clothes, anything that reminds him of Grace. The next thing he knows he is punching a man named Lucas Maddox as the masked man to the sounds of Eminem's 'The Way I Am.' He is so caught up in his rage that he forgot where he was. He doesn't even remember picking the song or why he chose it.

In this case his skills are both a blessing and a curse. Blessing that he is so good that he can do it in his sleep, and curse for the exact same reason.

"In life we must adapt or perish" says the masked man. "Life doesn't care how happy you were before, and it doesn't care what plans you have made. Something will happen to shake you up to the point where you can't control it anymore. When that happens, you have two options: adapt or perish. You can adapt to the situation life has put you in right now Maddox and tell me what you did with that video of you and Cindy getting it on, or you can perish."

"I don't have it" says Maddox through the pain.

"Fucking...tell me...right...now" says the masked man with a punch in between each word. "Did you know in some cultures they absolutely refuse to have their picture taken? They believe they lose a piece of their soul every time they do. If they're right, then you have a piece of Cindy's soul. Is that what you want?"

"No." I just wanted to-"

"I don't give a shit what you want" says the masked man to interrupt as he goes for his hammer. "I don't have a picture of you, but right now I own your soul. I decide if it stays here or goes straight to Hell. Now tell me." The masked man hammers Lucas' hand before he can answer, except with a scream. "Tell me." This time he hammers his foot. "Where is that God damn video?"

With that Cindy, Lucas' ex who hired Michael to retrieve the location of the video, bursts into the room to intervene.

"Stop. I don't want this" says Cindy.

"You hired me to get this information out of him. Now get out of my way."

"What kind of a man are you?" asks Cindy.

That phrase causes the masked man to flash back to that night in Afghanistan with the Jumbari family. Instead of sadness though, he is filled with anger and charges toward Cindy.

"You want to know what kind I am? I'm the one you hired for this to happen. Who the hell are you?" screams the masked man.

Cindy backs into a corner out of instinct and fear balling her eyes out. He raises his hand to hit her, but realizes what he is doing, and just stares at her. He looks over at Lucas, who is pretty much knocked stupid, and goes over to cut him loose. "You deal with him then" says the masked man. "Either you'll do anything to get that tape back, or you won't and he'll keep it. You can't have it both ways."

The masked man pushes Lucas out of the chair, grabs his supplies and leaves. He takes a few deep breaths outside of his car as he stares at his reflection. Instead of doing his prayer for forgiveness, he just drives away.

Michael walks into the warehouse and sees Father, as usual, waiting up to hear how the information gathering went. Instead of sharpening his knife, though, this time he is cleaning his old riffle.

"So how did it-"

"Fine" says Michael to interrupt, hoping that his Father won't try and dig deeper.

"Just fine? Nothing else to report?"

Michael stops because even if he didn't have his skills in reading people he would be able to tell that Father knows what happened.

"Why do you ask questions if you already know the answer?"

"Why do you feel the need to lie to me?" asks Father.

"I didn't lie. It went fine. Got in, got paid, and got out. No problem."

"That Cindy girl called. Said I better watch out because that masked guy snapped, and he didn't even get the information."

"She didn't want it anymore, she said so herself. I was beating it out of him, she caved in."

"That's it? You just beat it out of him?"

"What's wrong with that?"

"Nothing as long as you give him a chance to answer" says Father, "that's just not usually your style. And usually you know whether or not that's what the client wants."

"It worked for you. It can work for me. 'Hear, my son, your father's instruction, and forsake not your mother's teaching, for they are a graceful garland for your head and pendants for your neck.' Proverbs 1:8-9."

"Amen my son. But I don't like this anger I'm seeing in you, and it appears that it's coming out in your work."

"Isn't this what you wanted, Father? I'm here, I'm helping secure our place in Heaven, and I'm paying for what I did. What more do you want from me?"

"What I want is for your head to be in our work because when it is not, dangerous things happen. I don't care if you beat the holy hell out of some jack ass, I don't even care if you raise a hand to a woman, but if you go into every job thinking about the Jumbaris and about Grace, then you will get hurt, or get caught. That is worse than any other flashback or Cancer."

Michael and Father stare at each other. He can't help but think about how far their relationship has fallen from how it used to be. Unable to say anything, Michael decides to leave. As what seems to be the story of Michael's life, Father was right.

He did go into that job with his head and heart in the wrong place. His head was in Afghanistan and his heart is still with Grace. It's driving Michael crazy, to the point where he wants to forget about Grace, Hartley, the Jumbaris, about everything, even if just for a second. This is usually where he would go to the outdoor chapel that was built in honor of his Mother, but he knows he will still think of Grace. Not to mention that he doesn't want to visit that place when he is in such a sad and sorry state of mind. As much as Michael wants to avoid it, he knows of one place he can go to temporarily get away from the heart ache he feels, the local bar.

Two drinks in and Michael doesn't feel any different. Whether it's because he's never drunk to forget before and doesn't know how much it takes, or because the pain goes deeper than a tumbler of scotch is beyond him. But Michael does know that he wants to try. The way he sees it is that a hangover will feel better than the heart ache and memories, really anything would.

"Another one" says Michael to the Bartender, who notices that Michael's requests for drinks are coming quicker.

"Everything alright?" asks the bartender with very little sincerity.

"It'll be a little better once you hand me the next drink."

The bartender gladly obliges him. Two sips into his next drink and Michael is joined by a woman, even though companionship is the last thing he is looking for right now.

"What's your poison?" asks the lady. Michael ignores her, hoping she'll go away. "Not much for conversation. I like that."

"Good for you. I'm sure there's plenty of other guys in this bar who won't talk to you. So if you don't mind..."

"Wow. I'd hate to find out what she did to you."

"That obvious huh?" She nods in agreement. "I guess everybody can do my job as well as I can."

"Men come in here for one of two reasons," says the woman. "To forget or to pick up women. Either way a woman is involved."

"What makes you think it was her that did something to me?"

"That's always the case with you men. No decent man feels guilty enough to drink away their sorrows."

"No argument here" says Michael as he raises his glass to drink to her statement.

"But for fifty bucks, and one hour with me, I'll make you forget all about her."

"Fifty huh? Classy. Trust me lady, there's not enough hours in a year to make me forget about her."

"Come on babe" says the woman as she strokes Michael's hair.

The pet name is the last straw for Michael. He grabs her wrist and puts money in the woman's hand.

"Here's 100 dollars, now get the fuck away from me." says Michael as he shoves her wrist away. The woman is offended, as if she had never been turned down in her life, gives Michael a dirty look as she stuffs the bill in her bra and leaves.

"What are you? Some kind of faggot?" asks the bartender.

Michael grabs the bartender by the back of his neck and pulls him down until his face hits the bar. Michael cocks his fist back but it is stopped from behind. Michael turns and sees Grant Klein holding his harm.

"There are much better ways to get through your issues than beating up some ass hole Michael" says Grant. Michael lets go of the bartender who looks like he wants to fight. "Go pour another fruity drink."

"How did you know I was here?" asks Michael.

"Well you haven't been to the last few meetings. In my line of work that usually means the person decided to self-medicate. So I communicate with the owner, let him know if I'm looking for someone. Never thought I would have to give your description."

"Looks like I'm just letting everyone down."

"Why don't you tell me about it?"

"If I wanted to do that, Grant, I would have

come to a meeting. Now if you don't mind, I have to wait for another bartender to get a drink."

"Knock it off Michael. You're way too smart to think that you're going to find what you're looking for in a glass of booze. Tell me what's wrong."

"I don't owe you anything. I went to your meeting, thought I found what I wanted but I was wrong. Life isn't about what we say, what we get off our chest, it's about what we do."

"Hard to believe that's coming from you. The man who talks to God. What? You've given up on the power of prayer?"

"Sometimes I think it gave up on me."

Grant laughs.

"What the hell is so funny?" asks Michael.

"You're the kind of person I've been praying for." says Grant as he laughs a little more.

"You lost me," says Michael.

"You remind me a lot of myself when I was your age. You went through a terrible ordeal while serving, just like me, I found God, but I guess you always had God. I stumbled, now you're stumbling."

"You never said what you went through."

"It's my job to listen, Michael. To hear everyone else tell their story. Besides I told mine so many times I got sick of telling it. That's what people expected me to do. Report to my higher ups, share with my therapist, and communicate with my wife. It's amazing how many different words there are for sitting your ass down and talking." That gets Michael to snicker a little. "Anyway," continues Grant, "that's what I did. I kept telling my story, and to this day I don't know if I was bored and frustrated or just plain messed up from what I went through, but all it did was lead to me exploding and going to a bad place."

"And you felt alone" implies Michael.

"Not really. Everybody was there for me, they told me to let it out, and if I talked about how hard and terrible what I went through was it would all be okay. Most of them just smiled and nodded, nice enough to act like they understood, but that wasn't what I needed. It took me so many years and aggravation to figure out the key to moving forward with your life."

Grant takes a sip of his water while Michael waits for more.

"What is it?" asks Michael.

"I'm not telling you" says Grant somewhat smugly. "Everyone has to figure it out for themselves."

"You said that I am just like you. Shouldn't what worked for you, work for me as well?"

"Alright, if you want to know so badly I'll tell you. But I got to warn you, once people hear it; they tend to get frustrated because of how simple it is."

"Cut the bull shit Grant."

"If something is upsetting you" says Grant, who decides to hold with a dramatic pause. "Then just remove it from your life."

Michael is hoping for more, but Grant just continues to sip his drink. He was right about one thing; Michael is very frustrated right now.

"That's it?" asks Michael. "That's your great solution."

"Yep, that's about it."

"You've got to be kidding me. If something is bothering you, just stop doing it." says Michael with a mocking tone. "Is that what you tell everybody?"

"No. Actually you're the first. Didn't I say it would frustrate you?" Grant says through a laugh.

"Screw you." You honestly think it's that easy for everyone."

"Of course not. Just you. Well, and those who have someone to help them."

"It didn't work out with me and Grace."

"No shit" says Grant with sarcasm. "So what are you going to do about it?"

"There's nothing to do. I can't be who I am supposed to be around her."

"Michael I'm not your commanding officer so please cut that doing my duty shit. The only duty you have is to be happy and share that happiness with others. You're at your happiest when you're with Grace because you love her more than life itself."

"She came to one meeting with me. How the hell can you tell?"

"I could see it in your eyes. And let's just say I have a talent for reading people."

Grant uses a classic information getter move by pinching the space between Michael's thumb and index finger. Michael drops his glass on the ground out of the shock from the pinch, and drops his jaw from the shock of Grant's revelation.

"You were an information getter?"

Grant smiles, finishes his glass of water, stands up and pats Michael on the shoulder.

"Get your ass back to our meetings" says Grant as he exits the bar, leaving Michael with a lot to think about.

It's a beautiful summer day for graduation. Families and friends dressed up nicely to support their graduates gather in the outdoor venue of the University. Michael decides to stand in the back just in case this is a bad idea. Michael doesn't like working with a safety net like this, he always saw it as an act of half-assing the task put in front of him, but he's never dealt with a matter this close to his heart before. Michael watches the students enter hoping to catch a glimpse of Grace, but his attention is diverted when someone bumps into him.

"Excuse me" says Michael. He turns and sees that it is Vernon Clive.

"Oh no, I'm sorry." says Vernon.

Michael keeps the stare on Vernon, unsure if he can recognize him or not, so he gives him a little test.

"Do I know you?" asks Michael.

"I don't think so" says Vernon, "but if we have met I apologize for not remembering you." Vernon sees an old woman having trouble walking to her seat. "Excuse me please" he says to Michael. Vernon escorts the older woman to her seat with her family.

"I'll be damned," says Michael with a little chuckle.

"Thank you all for coming" says the master of ceremonies. "Today is truly a day of celebration, a day of moving forward. We will begin today's ceremony with our student speaker. Please welcome to the stage, graduating today with a degree in Psychology, Grace Everly."

Michael didn't know Grace was giving a speech, but he's not surprised. Nor is he surprised that even in a simple cap and gown Grace looks as lovely as ever.

"Thank you professor. Welcome family, friends, fellow graduates, faculty, and students. Well we did it, we finally made it through." As can be expected a loud applause erupts from all the excited graduates. "As professor Baranow said, today is a day to look forward. Some of us are thinking about how to get that job, some of us are contemplating whether or not we should continue on with school, and the rest are just worrying about what the future has in store for us. To those who are in the latter I say this, there is nothing wrong with that. There is that old saying, 'you can't live in the past' but sometimes I think that phrase keeps us from doing something very important, embracing the past. If we choose to embrace the past instead of living in it, then we can learn from it and it will help mold our future. Some of us have had difficult pasts, but that is what makes us who we are today. Every step, no matter how insignificant it may have seemed, whether it was a triumph or a failure, is what led you this day, as a successful student, or even just the amazing and unique person you are. I would like to conclude with something that someone very important to me once said: God's presence is everywhere. In a church, on a hill top, or simply in the presence of someone you care about, all we have to do is let him in our hearts.

I'm not saying everyone here should believe in God, you believe in who or whatever you want to. But be sure and keep an open mind and open heart to the world around you, because if you don't, you might miss out on something spectacular, like the past, present, or future. Thank you!"

Grace receives a standing ovation. Michael can't help but feel that maybe she was talking to him.

After the ceremony Michael wades through the

crowd of people to try and talk to Grace. When he finally sees her, she is taking a photo with an older man and woman. He realizes she is with her parents. Seeing how happy she is with them, Michael can't help but wonder if he should even try to come back into her life. Maybe she is doing just fine without him. He decides against it, and turns around to walk away.

"Michael?" yells Grace. When he turns and sees her walking toward him, that nervous feeling he had when they went on their first real date has come back. It's been weeks since he's seen her, but it felt like years to him. He once again has no idea what to say now. "I can't believe you came."

"That was a good speech," says Michael. They are both surprised that after weeks of no communication that is all he can say.

"Thanks" says Grace. "I don't know if you could tell, but I was talking about you."

"Yeah I figured that. Well I won't keep you from your parents" says Michael as he turns to walk away.

"Seriously? That's all you have to say to me? Nice speech and see ya? You know I don't let people get away without saying what they want to. Why are you here Michael?"

"I wanted to tell you something. But it's not important."

"Tell me."

"I don't want to ruin your day so-"

Grace embraces him to make him feel safe like he did for her.

"Just tell me."

"I meant what I said. This is who I am. Every minute of every hour of every day, except when I'm with you. I don't want to be this person anymore. I want to be the man that you see. I want to see through your eyes."

Michael begins to tear up. Grace looks into his eyes, wipes the tears away, and kisses him.

"Then be him." says Grace.

Michael kisses Grace for a while as if to make up for lost time.

"What are you doing today?"

"My parents are taking me to brunch to celebrate. Come with us."

"I want to, but there's something I got to do first." Grace gives him a concerned look. "Nothing like that. I'm meeting Grant to let him know everything is okay again. Can I come over tonight?"

"You better" says Grace.

She begins to walk away and Michael holds her hand for as long as he can. Michael has never felt so relieved in his life. He turns back to look at Grace but doesn't see her. He looks around and sees, what appears to be, Grace being ushered away. Michael doesn't like the look of this as he tries to get through the large crowd of people.

"Grace" yells Michael.

Grace quickly turns but the person next to her forces her to keep walking forward. That's when Michael notices the person has a gun pointed at Grace's side. Michael is now pushing his way past people, but there are just so many. A car pulls up to a curb and Grace is pushed in. The person next to her follows and closes the door. Michael is sprinting with all he has toward the car. The person looks out the car window and Michael can see that it is Wyatt, the associate of Seth Zern, who arrogantly waves at Michael with his scarred hand as the car takes off. Michael doesn't know what to do, but he does know where he can get some answers.

He opens the door of the warehouse so hard that he knocks it off its hinges.

"Father. Where are you?"

"Over here son" says Father. "I think this video message is what you're looking for."

Michael presses the play button on the lap top, and Seth Zern appears with Grace sitting in a chair.

"Hello Michael. By now you've probably figured out two things. One is that we have this lovely lady in our possession, and two, that no one says no to me. Here is another Machiavelli quote I like: 'It is better to be feared than loved if you cannot be both.' I offered you the chance to get paid very well to do what you do best and you turn me down. But hey, I'm a reasonable man. You don't want to work exclusively for me, all I want is one job and then you're done, and you'll get to be with this lovely lady again. You'll find a file with everything you need to get the job done. You have twenty-four hours. I have to warn you about something Michael, I'm a patient man, but Wyatt isn't. Should you take longer...well... he'll take his frustrations out on her." Wyatt steps into the camera shot and slaps Grace. "Twenty-four hours Michael. See you soon."

The video ends and in a fit of rage Michael picks up the lap top and throws it as he screams. He then grabs Father and puts him up against the wall.

"Did you know he would do this?" asks Michael.

"How could you even ask that?"

"Did you know?"

"No son. I don't want this to happen to you."

Michael knows that no matter whose fault it is this is not the time to lose his mind with anger. He picks up the file and begins to read it.

"David Durst. Owner and operator of 3D defense. According to this he is on the verge of inventing a new cyber defense system. If it works as well as to be expected it will revolutionize government defense, make top secret data bases practically impenetrable. This sort of thing could be worth billions."

"Probably why Zern is willing to go this far" says Father. "If this is true, then I guarantee the government gave him all kinds of security details until he finishes it. You might as well go after the president. There's no way you can get in the same room as him, let alone tie him down and get the information out of him." Michael doesn't even acknowledge Father, but Father can tell that the wheels are spinning in Michael's head, formulating a plan. "What are you going to do son?"

"He wants someone to get information from; I'll give it to him"

CHAPTER 18

In the past this kind of rage has caused Michael to fall into the fog. Not knowing how he got from one place to another or even what he did in between point A or B. But for the first time in his life the rage is making him as clear as ever. The irony doesn't escape Michael. He spent the last year wondering if he should be the masked man anymore, and now, more than ever, he needs him. While it was Michael who joined the army and learned how to fight, it is the masked man that can take any situation and bring an extra level of intensity to it. It makes Michael wonder if it was the masked man getting the info out of Lucas Maddox or was it just him?

Putting on the mask itself doesn't mean much to Michael. It was always just a way to cover his identity when he had to. It's when he opens his eyes and looks through the goggles that is the trigger. That makes the transformation from Michael to the masked man complete. Like the old saying goes, the eyes are the window to the soul. But what happens when the windows are covered? There is nothing but darkness.

Seth Zern seems very comfortable with having a woman in his possession. It's as if it is another day of work for him. It makes Grace wonder what sins are buried in his past. Here are two men with very similar lives, put on similar paths, but turned out so different. They both went into the military; both used it as a way to succeed financially. Yet one is driven by greed and power while the other is driven by faith and justice.

"This is a very tricky situation," says Seth to Grace. "Please believe me when I say this Miss..."

"Go to Hell."

Wyatt grabs Grace by the hair.

"Now Wyatt we must be polite to our guest, even if she won't be." Wyatt relinquishes. "What I was going to say is that we take no pleasure in this. But we need Michael's talents to get that information on the latest 3D defense technology or everything I worked for will be gone. I can't allow that."

"Do you actually believe your own bull shit?"

"A lady, as beautiful as you, should not use language like that" he says as he strokes Grace's hair. "I'll tell you what, after I get my information, I'll get you a beautiful dress, with some beautiful jewelry, and take you to a pent house with the most beautiful view in the world."

Seth is now stroking Grace's face.

"Actually, I've already seen the most beautiful view in the whole world."

With that Grace bites Seth's finger. He screams in pain and manages to pull away.

"You ugly bitch."

Seth punches Grace and she is knocked to the floor. He goes to do it again but is stopped by Wyatt.

"Mr. Zern. There is a car pulling into the compound."

Seth gets up to look at the monitor and sees just that. As the car gets further, he can see that the masked man is driving and there is someone in the back with a hood over their head. The car screeches to a halt and the masked man gets out and looks around. When he sees the camera, he points to the person in the back and runs away.

"Rome you take some men and go check on that."

"Yes Mr. Zern" says Rome as he exits.

"Wyatt, cuff our rude guest to the chair. She wants to act like an animal; we'll treat her like one."

"With pleasure" says Wyatt.

Rome leads some men to the compound. Part of what made him one of Seth's closest associates is that he is as cautious as he is intense. He wouldn't be surprised if Michael rigged a couple of grenades to go off in the car to help take out a few men. He forces one of the workers to check out the undercarriage of Michael's car. With no bombs in sight, the worker slowly opens the car as if the speed would make a difference between a trap blowing up or not.

"All clear" says the worker after he opens the door all the way.

Now Rome is a beacon of confidence as he strolls to the car. He sees that the person is tied to the passenger seat with a note.

"Here is your direct source to the technology. Let Grace go out the back where I'll be waiting, and then I'll tell you how he built his new technology. Even if you don't believe me, you have him to question" says Rome, reading the note aloud, which makes him and the others laugh. "That's what I love about dumb religious fucks; they think peoples' word means something."

They grab the hooded person and bring him into the room where Grace is held.

"Where is Michael?" asks Seth.

"He's waiting for her outside? He'll tell us everything after we let her go, or after Durst tells us everything. See?" says Rome pointing to the security monitor to show the masked man waiting outside.

"Well then, you know what to do" says Seth.

"No. Michael, run." screams Grace before she is gagged by Wyatt.

"He's mine." says Wyatt. "I want what's coming to me after what that son of a bitch did to my hand."

"Wyatt I need you here to get the info out of Durst. Come on, you may not get his head, but I'll let you have the next best thing" he says as he motions to Grace. Wyatt smiles an evil grin and nods in agreement.

"Rome, take the men out back and handle him."

Without a word Rome does as he is told and leads

the rest of the workers outside. He is a man of few words after all. He gets outside and only takes a couple steps before he shoots the masked man twice in the chest.

Grace cries through the gag. It's hard to believe that after all Michael went through in his life his story ends just like that, with two steps and two shots.

Rome motions for the workers to get rid of the body. Four men lift the masked man up onto their shoulders and begin to walk away. They stop when they hear a 'cling' sound, like metal hitting cement. One of the workers finds the source of the sound in a vague looking object. Before he can even pick up the object the men are blinded by a light. It was a flash bang grenade.

"What the hell?" screams Rome, who was lucky enough to have his back turned to the grenade. He can't believe his eyes when the masked man stands up. So much so that he forgot he had more shots in his gun. By the time he raises his gun the masked man knocks it out of his hand.

"Mr. Zern, he's back up and fighting Rome" says Wyatt.

"What? I thought Rome put two in him."

"He did."

The masked man punches Rome in the face and the two begin fighting. Rome knows how to fight, he is able to land a few shots, but the masked man is dominating Rome.

"Damn it. Wyatt, shoot the first thing that comes through that door."

"But what if it's-"

"The first thing" screams Seth. "Get up, Durst." Seth drags the hooded person to their feet.

In an act of desperation Rome jumps on the back of the masked man. He powers through and flips Rome over his head. Rome managed to take the mask with him on the way down.

"Who are you?" asks Rome before he is kicked in the head.

"Mr. Zern. It wasn't Michael. It's a diversion."

"What?" says Seth.

The person in the hood sidekicks Seth and rips off the hood to reveal that it was Michael all along.

"Surprise" says Michael.

"Shoot him Wyatt" says Seth half out of breath. "Kill him."

Wyatt just stares at Michael, practically salivating at the chance for revenge.

"He's not going to do that. Aren't you Wyatt?"

Wyatt stares at his hand with the scar on it from when Michael, as the masked man, stabbed him. Wyatt tosses the gun away, and takes out a buck knife.

"No." screams Seth.

"You wouldn't understand Zern. You're not a soldier" says Michael as he takes out his switch blade.

Michael and Rome stare each other down. Not just waiting for one to make the first move, but also as if telling the other that only one of them is walking away from this alive.

"I'm going to cut you into enough little pieces to mail home, starting with your hand" says Wyatt. "Then I'll unwind by fucking your girl."

"Come and get what you deserve" says Michael.

Wyatt screams like a warrior and charges at Michael. One thing the army taught Michael is that when in a knife fight, you must be patient. Like in most sports games it is the best defense that wins the day. Because of that lesson Michael is letting Wyatt make the first move. The other thing about fighting someone with a weapon is that he knows his opponent will use it. Every swipe and lunge that Wyatt makes, Michael answers with a smooth perry. It's like watching a video of his last few information gathering sessions for Michael. He can see that Wyatt is fighting with rage and not a level head.

Something that Michael learned from his Father is that knife wielders and snipers share one thing in common, they only get one shot.

"Don't they teach you how to knife fight in Russia?" says Michael as he manages to create some space between them. "Or are you all pussies who hide behind guns?"

Wyatt lunges at Michael who sidesteps and stabs Wyatt in the wrist causing him to drop his buck knife. In one motion Michael puts Wyatt in a choke hold and repeatedly stabs him in the back with his switch blade. Wyatt slowly falls to his knees while choking on his blood and gasping for air. Michael gently lays Wyatt on his back. In his last act of toughness Wyatt smiles at Michael as if thanking him for one last good fight, and dies.

"You're next Zern" says Michael as he turns with his bloody knife in hand.

During the fight Zern grabbed the gun Wyatt threw away and is pointing it at Grace.

"All you had to do was work with me Michael. Then none of this would have happened. I succeeded in life by eliminating everyone's options except the one that benefited me. I have a gun pointed at the woman you love Michael. So what are your options?"

Michael takes a knee and does the sign of the cross.

"Father, I ask that you dispense your justice from above now."

"Are you fucking serious? I got some bad news for you Michael. You think because you say a few prayers every day that you and your Father are so much better than us-"

Before Seth can finish his statement he is shot in the head from outside. Grace can't believe her eyes. Michael walks over to Seth's body and stands over it to watch the life go out of his eyes.

"Not yet, but I can be." Michael runs to Grace, takes the gag off and kisses her. "Are you okay?"

"Yeah. How did this happen?"

Michael shows Grace his cell phone was on. He looks out the window and waves to Father who was perched on top of the adjoining building.

It was very easy for Grace to fall asleep. She went through the physical and emotional grind in one day. It also helps that Michael is there with her, holding her and keeping her safe. Michael looks over the mirror in Grace's room and likes what he sees.

Michael goes to Grant's office to thank him, even though there aren't enough words to express how grateful he is.

"Thank you Grant."

"Glad I could help. How is she?"

"She's doing fine. She is one tough woman."

"Good. She'll keep you on your toes. And how are you?"

"I want to say fine, good, great, but it doesn't feel like that. I guess I'm afraid I'll just go back to that dark place to become the masked man and disappoint Grace."

"Want the harsh truth Michael?"

"Is there any other kind?"

"That feeling isn't going to go away. The battle won't be won, and the war won't ever end. God, I was in that mask for less than an hour and I feel like less the person I was before. I don't know how the hell you did it all those years."

"I didn't. It changed me in more ways than I can count."

"But remember this Michael; while the mask can change you, it is you who puts it on every time. And you have the power to change that."

Michael thinks about it for a while, gets up and hugs Grant, and leaves without saying anything. No words are needed. Michael is going to be doing enough talking about where he is going next.

Michael has walked through the door to his warehouse thousands of times, but this time feels different. It's like he's entering an unfamiliar place, and it seems smaller. Michael doesn't know exactly why, it's the home he grew up in, it's where he experienced every milestone in his life, he went through tragedies and triumphs, but for some reason it's like a different door he is walking through.

"Hello my son. I'm glad you're home. There is something I need to tell you. You were right. We shouldn't have worked with Zern. He was not for us or our cause. Perhaps I should have guessed when your name is the God of Chaos right?" Michael just keeps the stare. "I guess I just can't read people as well as I used to, but you can. That's why I want you to start interacting with the clients now. I'll find them, but you go with me to meet them. And if you feel something is off then I'll just listen to you automatically. No questions asked." Michael doesn't respond at all, but it's obvious he is holding something back. "Well say something Michael?"

"No," says Michael.

"Michael, you should learn how to do this. I won't be around much longer."

"I'm not saying no to that. I'm saying no to you."

"What, you don't want me in the business anymore? I'm sorry about what happened to Grace-"

"I'm saying no to it all Father" screams Michael. "No. I'm out."

"Son, you went through something very difficult."

"I spoke with your doctor. He says he'll be surprised if you don't live to be 100, and didn't mention anything about cancer."

"I know how this looks, Michael. But you have to see it from my point of view. You were going to make a huge mistake."

"It's over Father. I can't do this anymore."

"Michael you've said that before, but we both know you always end up coming back to what you know and love."

"Let me tell you something you don't know. When I wake up in the morning I go right to the mirror and I hope to see someone different. That everything I did was just a bad dream, but I don't. I just see what I have become. Every day I try and make that enough, but now I know it never will be. I want to like what I see in my reflection but I can't because what I see is what you created.

I'm not talking about my life, I'm talking about what you and Hartley made me into, a mindless and soulless machine. Do you know what I do after every job? I beg for forgiveness just like you taught me. But I finally realized that no matter how hard or how often I pray that God won't forgive me, because I'm not even trying to change. I'm living a hollowed faith of convenience. But I know I can change, at least when I'm not with you. I thought I was doing some good in the world, but I'm not. I'm just your way of doing what you believe is justice because all you see is Mom being killed. You taught me many good things Father, I know I wouldn't have my faith if it wasn't for you, but you also taught me to not feel. Maybe that's good enough for you, but not for me, not since I met Grace. She asked me to leave, and that's what I'm doing. I'm out. Not to spite you, but so when I wake up, I won't have to look in the mirror, I'll just look over at her, and know I did something right."

Father looks at Michael. Watching the tears run down his face, practically out of breath from finally letting it all out.

"You really think cutting me out of your life is going to make you feel better?" He turns his back on Michael. "You want to go? Go. I know you'll be back. No matter how much you don't like this anymore, it's a part of your life."

"That's not how I do things anymore. If I don't like something, then I'm cutting it out of my life. Good bye Father."

Michael turns and leaves. Now it's as if he doesn't even recognize the door anymore. The sound of the door closing behind him makes Father turn around.

"He'll be back" he says to himself with confidence. But that confidence goes away when he sees the mask left on the table.

The sound of the car humming along on the interstate is music to Michael's ears. He looks over at Grace in the passenger seat and she smiles back at him. Neither of them can believe this is really happening. Grace is starting her dream career with the man she loves, and Michael gets a fresh start.

"Do you have that weird feeling like I do right now?" asks Michael.

"What do you mean?"

"I don't know. It's like with every mile I have this pulling feeling inside me."

"It's just nerves babe. Suck it up" Grace says sarcastically.

"Wait. I know what it is" says Michael as he makes a quick turn.

"Where are we going?"

"There's one thing I'm going to miss."

Michael stares at the one thing he knows he can't take with him to his new life in Chicago that he wants to. He knows the urge to be the masked man once again, his remorse for what happened in Afghanistan, and curiosity about his Father will follow him wherever he goes, but a sunset at the outdoor chapel is something he has to say goodbye to.

Luckily he has the one thing that will top all that, the love of Grace.

"It doesn't have to be goodbye forever" says Grace.

"Yes it does" says Michael. "But that's fine with me."

"How can you be so calm about this?"

Michael smiles at Grace and gets out his I-touch and docking player. So many times he used that for something that caused him emotional pain. But now he is using it to move forward with his life. He puts on 'Fly Me To the Moon' and dances with Grace. The feeling of being safe is there between the two of them, and hopefully, God willing, it will stay forever.

The End.

www.ingramcontent.com/pod-product-compliance
Lightning Source LLC
LaVergne TN
LVHW090612110826
845146LV00001B/353

* 9 7 9 8 2 3 4 0 9 4 5 9 9 *